For Rosie

Copyright © 1992 by Catherine and Laurence Anholt

First U.S. edition 1992
Published in Great Britain in 1992 by Walker Books Ltd., London.

Library of Congress Cataloging-in-Publication Data:

Anholt, Catherine.
Kids / by Catherine and Laurence Anholt.—1st U.S. edition
Summary: Illustrations and rhyming text present the traits, activities, and
feelings of many different children.
[1. Children—Fiction. 2. Individuality—Fiction. 3. Stories in rhyme.]
I. Anholt, Laurence. II. Title.
PZ8.3.A5492Ki 1992   91-58739
[E]—dc20
ISBN 1-56402-097-5

10 9 8 7 6 5 4 3 2

Printed in Hong Kong

The pictures in this book were done in watercolor and ink.

Candlewick Press
2067 Massachusetts Avenue
Cambridge, Massachusetts 02140

KIDS

by Catherine and Laurence Anholt

CANDLEWICK PRESS
CAMBRIDGE, MASSACHUSETTS

We are the kids!

Big kids, small kids, tiny kids, tall kids

Happy kids, grumpy kids, skinny kids, dumpy kids

Look out, here we come!

Slow kids, quick kids, healthy kids, sick kids

Smooth kids, hairy kids, cute kids, scary kids

What are kids like?

Kids are silly, kids are funny,

Kids have noses that are runny.

Some kids wash but some are muddy,

Both kinds have a favorite buddy.

What do kids look like?

Freckles and buttons and ink on their skirts,

Glasses and smiles and hanging-out shirts.

Kids put their left foot
where the right one should be,

They have gaps in their teeth
and a cut on each knee.

What do kids do?

mix

mess

muddle

comfort

kiss

cuddle

laugh

leap

lick

poke

push

pick

scratch

scream

scrawl

break

bellow

bawl

Where do kids hide?

Seven in a bed, six in a box,

Five behind curtains, four behind clocks,

Three in a tree, two in a hole.

Here is a kid who hid in some coal.

What's in a kid's pocket?

rubber band

stones and sand

handkerchief

pretty leaf

jam and bread

someone's head

pieces of string

another thing

What do kids make?

Houses with blankets,

Mountains on stairs,

Seas out of carpets,

Trains out of chairs.

What scares kids?

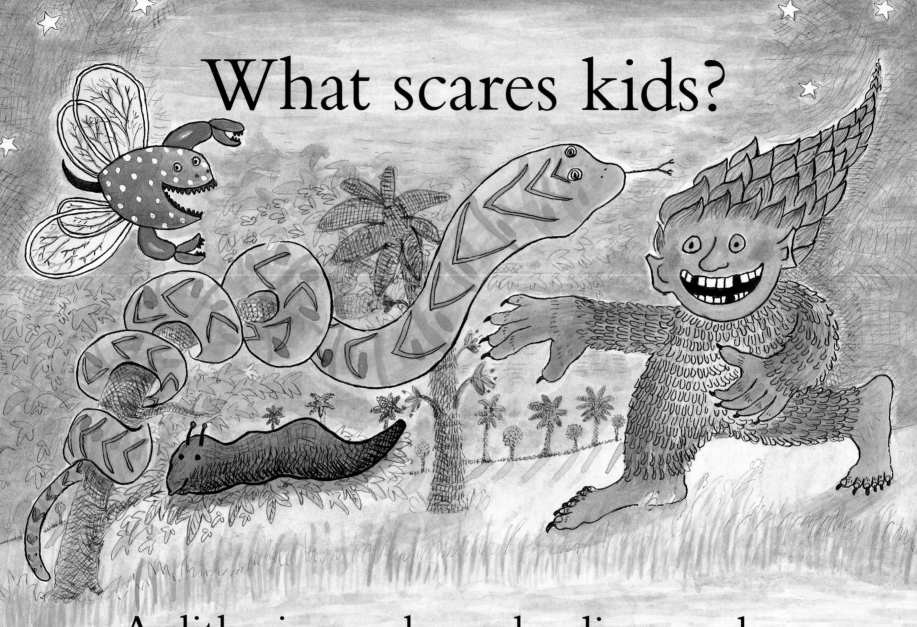

A slithering snake and a slippery slug,
A girl-eating ghoul and a boy-biting bug,

A gremlin, a goblin, a ghost in the dark,
A tiny black spider, a giant white shark.

What are kids' secrets?

A ladybug in a matchbox,

A letter under a bed,

A horrible pie in a horrible place,

A fort behind a shed.

What are nasty kids like?

They pull your hair, they call you names,
They tell you lies, they spoil your games,
They draw on walls, scream on the floor.
Nasty kids want more, more, more.

What are nice kids like?

They make you laugh, they hold your hand,
Nice kids always understand.
They share their toys, they let you play,
They chase the nasty kids away.

What do kids dream of?

A ladder to the moon,

A candy tree in bloom,

Riding a flying fish,

Having anything they wish.

What do moms and dads do?

Neaten, carry, clean and cook,

Wash the baby, read a book, then...

Kiss us when

It's nearly night:

Dads and moms

Switch off the light.